DEDICATION

To my students: past, present and future, you are powerful beyond measure!

To my daughter Jasmine who inspired me to co-author this book, I love you

unconditionally. Always remember, your voice matters

and everything you need is already inside of you!

ISBN: 979-8-9882234-1-2

Christina's CommUNITY Cues

CANDICE CHRISTINA AND JASMINE CHRISTINA

Today is Christina's first day at Shining Star Elementary School.
She is assigned to Ms. Peach's 3rd grade class.
Christina is terrified!

She had been at her previous school since kindergarten. She will have a new teacher and have to make friends all over again.

Walking up to the classroom, Christina sees her new teacher greeting each student with a warm smile and a hug at the door.

6 Now, Christina is starting to feel more relaxed.

The bell rings and everyone takes their seats.
Ms. Peach welcomes the class and asks each
student to introduce themselves.

Nervously, Christina stands up and says, "My name is Christina and I have one baby brother. I love the color purple and sushi rolls." Immediately another student yells out, "I really love sushi rolls too!"

Without even thinking, Christina gives him the AGREE cue.
At her other school students and teachers always used
CommUNITY Cues to share answers and ideas with each other.

They used CommUNITY Cues outside during recess,
in the cafeteria and even in music class.
Using them made every person feel connected
no matter where they were.

Ms. Peach thanks Christina for sharing as the class lines up for lunch. Ms. Peach whispers in Christina's ear, "Today, you are going to eat lunch in the classroom with me."

12

Christina's tummy turns upside down and
inside out.

She wrinkles her face as she stands in line worrying about why
Ms. Peach could possibly want to have lunch with her.
She thinks that she is in BIG t-r-o-u-b-l-e!

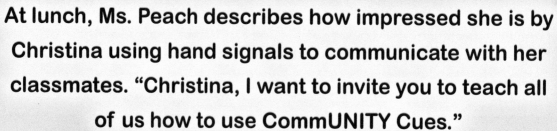

At lunch, Ms. Peach describes how impressed she is by Christina using hand signals to communicate with her classmates. "Christina, I want to invite you to teach all of us how to use CommUNITY Cues."

As Christina eats her lunch, Ms. Peach shares her
excitement about having her at Shining Star Elementary.
Christina knows her previous teachers would be
so proud of how her first day is going.

At recess, Christina makes some new friends while playing tag.
A classmate says, "playing hide-and-seek is
way better than playing tag!"

Christina
RESPECTFULLY
DISAGREES.

"There she goes again with those hand signals!" her classmate shouts. Christina explains she was RESPECTFULLY DISAGREEING because tag is her favorite game to play, not hide-and-seek.

Back inside the school, Ms. Peach invites the class to write and draw about their summer break.

"I love my new class", Christina smiles to herself as she draws.

At home that evening, Christina thinks of all the CommUNITY Cues she used while at her other school and how she can share them at Shining Star Elementary.

"I got it!" Christina thinks to herself. "I can share one CommUNITY Cue each day in class! I will just keep adding more and more until they know them all, just like me!"

21

The next day, Christina gives her classmates a **GOOD JOB** cue whenever they answer questions correctly or show kindness. Before the day is over, each student in class is doing the same thing!

Remembering Christina's CommUNITY Cues, Ms. Peach silently
AGREES with Mr. Sanchez who is standing across the hall
when he says his kids will have indoor recess because
it is raining outside.

After recess, Christina uses her QUESTION cue while asking Ms. Peach for help with her math.

At the end of the lesson, Christina models the **MORE DETAIL** cue inviting Ms. Peach to further explain the steps to addition.

During math the next week, Ms. Peach asks Christina
to come to the board to solve an addition problem.
Once Christina finishes, she turns around and sees most of
her classmates using their RESPECTFULLY DISAGREE cue.

$$\begin{array}{r} 82 \\ + 18 \\ \hline 910 \end{array}$$

Christina instantly checks her work but cannot find the mistake. She puts up her QUESTION cue to ask for help and a classmate explains to her that she forgot to regroup.

Christina quickly reworks the problem.

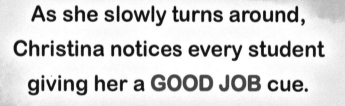

As she slowly turns around, Christina notices every student giving her a **GOOD JOB** cue.

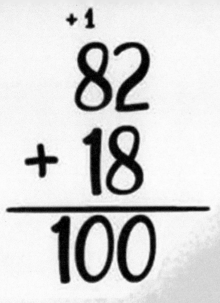

$$\begin{array}{r} {}^{+1}\\ 82\\ +\ 18\\ \hline 100 \end{array}$$

She beams with pride!

Ms. Peach sees Principal Richmond walking down the hall. She invites him to visit her classroom and see her brilliant students in action.

As Principal Richmond walks around Ms. Peach's classroom, he is thrilled that everyone is working so well together on their math problems. Instantly, he notices a student AGREEING about an answer and asking the group for MORE DETAIL.

"For the first time in Shining Star history, every student in every classroom is fully engaged. It is because they are using CommUNITY Cues. Ms. Peach, I think Christina is onto something here!" Principal Richmond exclaims.

"I cannot believe it!" Christina says excitedly.
"The whole school is using the strategy I shared!"

Ms. Peach announces to Principal Richmond and the class that Christina is the Shining Star of the Month! All the students run up to hug Christina. "Now this is what commUNITY is all about", says Principal Richmond.

About the Authors

Candice Christina, is a native of Cincinnati, OH and currently lives in Louisville, KY. She is the proud mother of Jasmine C. Hardin, and enjoys traveling, creating art, and spending time with her family and friends. Candice is an alumna of Spelman College and also a proud member of Delta Sigma Theta Sorority, Inc. Named a "Hero in Education" and a "Teacher of Excellence", Candice has led students and teachers across all grade levels in the Jefferson County Public Schools (JCPS) system and throughout greater Kentucky. Her experiences as a parent and teacher inspired *Christina's CommUNITY Cues*, to help students and others find and share their voice. Candice continues her advocacy of children and teachers through her company, Level Up Consulting, LLC.

Jasmine Christina, a native of Louisville, KY is a star student with a love for unicorns, sushi, and traveling. She enjoys spending time with her family, playing with friends, and participating in basketball, gymnastics, and swimming. Jasmine believes that every person has a voice and every voice has value. Jasmine wants to inspire each reader to have the courage and confidence to share their ideas with others, just like Christina! She will continue to make an impact by encouraging others to use CommUNITY Cues to share their thoughts and make friends!

Visit Level Up Consulting at **321levelup.com** to learn more!

CommUNITY Cue Corner

Add On

Agree

Because Clap

Answer

Comment

More Detail

Confused

Good Job

Disagree

Question

Slow Down

Repeat

Vocabulary

Made in the USA
Columbia, SC
20 July 2024

38546640R00022